the
nature
of GOD

Ocean
Adventures

Introduction

"Hey, I got a Tako (Ta-co)!" said the young man as he swam back to our boat. In his hands was an octopus! "Get in the water so I can hand it to you."

Once it was in my hands (and all over my arms and chest), I was fascinated by how the octopus felt and moved. It was squishy and slippery, like it was a limp soggy body—but when it tried to push away from me, it felt hard, with incredible strength and power. God must have had fun creating such a unique and funny-looking creature.

God has blessed me with many amazing wildlife experiences like this one off the coast of Maui. But they didn't happen by sitting at home—I had to get outside so God could show me his incredible natural world. My hope is that this book will not only help you understand the majesty and creativity of our great Creator, but also inspire you to explore and experience the nature of God for yourself.

—Peter Schriemer

What Is a Habitat?

Ever wanted to be an explorer or an adventurer? I hope so. God filled our planet with amazing creatures for us to discover and enjoy. Each animal and plant is designed in a special way to serve a special purpose in God's natural world.

Plants and animals are made to live together in places we call habitats. A habitat is a space where plants and animals interact in a way that keep things in balance and makes it possible for life to exist. A coral reef, a shoreline, and a jungle are all different habitats.

Different animals have different needs, which is why there are so many different habitats in the world. No matter what type of habitat, all creatures need certain things to be just right in order for them to live in that habitat.

Habitats Provide Creatures with:

- Oxygen (in the right amounts)
- Suitable Temperatures
- Food
- Water
- Shelter
- Area to Raise Young

The Huge Ocean

The Pacific Ocean is the biggest body of water in the world. It covers one-third of the earth's surface! It is so big that all the continents could fit inside it—with room left over! If you were a creature living in the ocean, what would it be like?

First, you'd need to be able to get freshwater. Some creatures are designed to get freshwater out of the food they eat. Others are able to remove the salt from the ocean water they drink.

Most living creatures need oxygen, because oxygen gives the body's cells the energy to function. Creatures like fish get oxygen out of the water by using their gills. Animals like whales come up to the surface and breathe air like people.

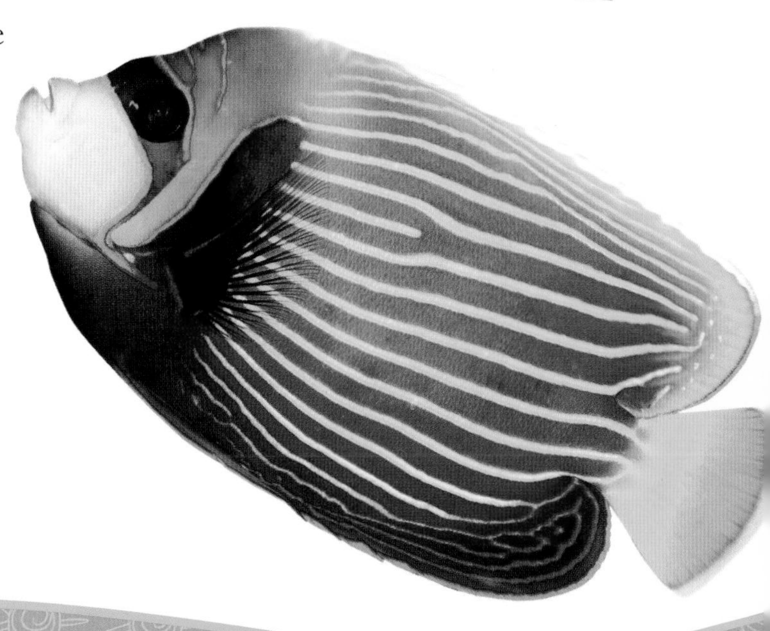

Ocean plants live near the surface because they need sunlight to grow. Most ocean animals live near the surface too, where they can eat plants or hunt for food.

Temperature is also a big deal for survival in the ocean. Creatures like sea turtles are cold-blooded. This means they get their body heat from the environment around them. Other creatures, like dolphins, are warm-blooded. They need to keep their bodies a consistent temperature all the time. To do that, they have an extra layer of fat on their bodies to keep them warm!

Ninety percent of all ocean life can be found in coastal ocean habitats. Are you ready to dive into this watery world? Let's go!

The Coral Reef

Coral reefs are filled with amazing creatures. Hawaii has one of the most unique coral reef systems on the plane Coral reefs are called "the rain forests of the ocean" because they are home to 25% of all ocean creatures—even though they take up only about 2% of the ocean.

Corals are actually colonies or groups of tiny creatures called polyps building little homes out of limestone. When there are a lot of them, you get unusual coral structures. The amazing colors come from algae growin on the coral.

Coral reefs need warm temperatures and sunlight. Healt coral reefs can get big. In fact, the Great Barrier Reef in Australia is the biggest structure on earth built by living organisms. It can be seen from space!

Sea Urchin

This spiky ball is a creature called a sea urchin. The spikes on its body are for protection and camouflage. Sea urchins get around by moving their spikes and using teeny-tiny tube feet that help them hold onto the ocean floor.

The sea urchin's mouth is on the bottom of its body. Being omnivores, they eat small animals, plants, and decaying matter from the ocean floor or among the corals.

Sea Cucumber

Like earthworms in your backyard, God gave sea cucumbers the important job of cleaning up their habitat. They eat everything in their path. They don't have brains like you and me, and in parts of the deep ocean, there are large groups of these brainless tubes grazing on the microscopic bounty of the sea.

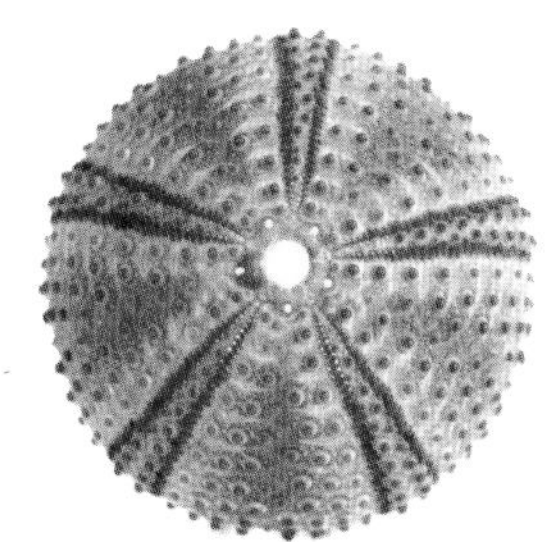

When threatened by a predator, a sea cucumber shoots some of its guts into the water to distract the predator! Then it regrows its internal organs and is just fine.

Triggerfish

The state fish of Hawaii is the reef triggerfish. You can identify many types of fish by the way they swim and thi is one of them. Triggerfish move their fins in a wave-like pattern to swim through the water.

When the triggerfish is threatened, it quickly swims dow to a crevice in the coral and sticks out a "trigger" type spine from its top fin. Using the trigger, it wedges itself tight against the coral. That way a predator will have a hard time reaching it.

Puffer Fish

Puffer fish may be slow swimmers, but God gave them a great defense. They can swallow huge amounts of water and become several times their normal size! When the puffer fish does this, predators think they are too big to eat.

That's not all God gave the puffer fish. Puffer fish have a poison in their bodies for defense, and they usually have rough or spiky skin to discourage predators from eating them!

If puffer fish are out of the water, they can quickly inflate with air.

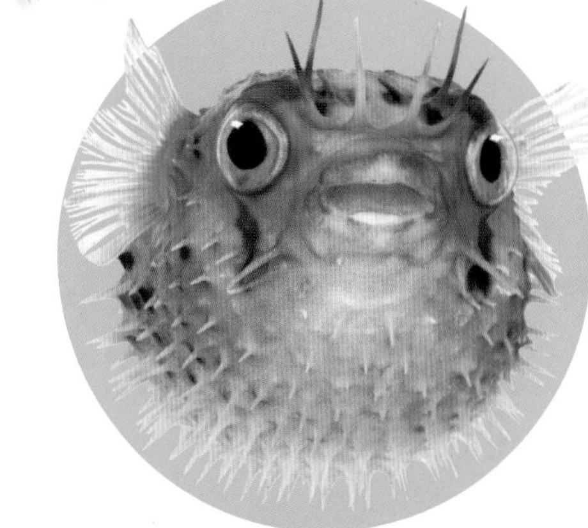

Octopus

Did you know octopuses can almost instantly change color? Even faster than a chameleon, they can blend into their background and hide in plain sight.

God gave octopuses super-special pigment cells and specialized muscles in their skin. This allows them to mimic the colors, patterns, and even textures of their surroundings! Predators, like sharks, can swim close by an octopus and never see it.

Octopuses can also squirt a cloud of ink at an attacker. The ink not only blocks the predator's view, but also dulls its ability to smell the octopus and track it down.

When it comes to escaping, octopuses are fast swimmers. They can also squeeze their oddly shaped bodies into very tight places to stay out of reach.

If caught in something or injured, octopuses can regrow tentacles later with no problem!

Crazy Cool FACT!

Humpback Whale

Humpback whales are some of the biggest animals on earth, sometimes reaching 45 feet long and weighing up to 112,000 pounds! They may be huge, but just like all other mammals, whales are warm-blooded, give live birth, and breathe air just like you and me.

Whales don't breathe through a nose on their face like we do. Instead, God put their nose (called a blowhole) on the top of their body. They breathe when they come up to the surface (called spouting). Spouting is a great way to spot whales. You can see these huge blasts of water from miles away.

Whales are divided into two major groups: toothed whales and baleen whales. Humpbacks have baleen—which are big thick brushes on their upper jaw to filter out the water from their food. It's like having a comb in your mouth instead of those pearly white teeth!

Along the coast of Alaska, humpbacks gulp big mouthfuls of water along with schools of small fish and krill. They then filter out the water using their baleen and swallow the small creatures. They can literally eat 2,000 pounds of food in a day!

After eating their fill during the summer, humpbacks swim the several thousand-mile trip from Alaska to Hawaii where their babies are born. At birth, baby humpbacks can be 16 feet long and weigh 4,000 pounds!

45 feet!

Crazy Cool FACT!

All whale tails (called flukes) are unique—just like your fingerprint! Scientists can identify an individual whale by the pattern and markings on its fluke.

Green Turtle

Green turtles are one of the biggest sea turtles and can grow longer than three feet and weigh more than 300 pounds! They spend most of their lives in the ocean, but mama turtles come out of the water to lay about 100 eggs in springtime at the exact same beach every year.

It is marvelous how God gave the turtle the ability to know which way is north, kind of like it has a compass, so it can make decisions on which way to go. God gave this amazing ability to the turtle, because he knows exactly what it needs to survive and reproduce.

nesting turtle

Crazy Cool FACT!

While the green turtle's eggs are in the sand, temperature is a big deal. Warm weather produces girl turtles, and cool weather produces boy turtles!

Bottlenose Dolphin

Bottlenose dolphins are very intelligent. Being very social creatures, they love interaction and communicate with each other through a system of squeaks, chirps, and clicks. Dolphins are even able to identify each other by the sounds of their voices.

Dolphins use sound to sense what's ahead of them. They make a click noise and the sound wave travels through the water, bouncing off objects, and returning to the dolphin. This is called echolocation. It helps them spot predators and find fish to eat. God provides each creature with what it needs to survive.

Wild bottlenose dolphins have been known to save people's lives by attacking and chasing off sharks.

Crazy Cool FACT!

Formation of an Island

Most of the seafloor of the Pacific Ocean is a massive piece of land called the "Pacific Plate," which moves about two to four inches a year. As the land moves over a spot deeper in the earth where lava forms, volcanoes can punch through the land and create an island. The Hawaiian Islands are actually the tops of enormous volcanic mountains that go down more than three miles to the ocean floor.

Whether you're a creature of the land or the ocean in the Hawaiian Islands, you need freshwater. Some ocean creatures filter freshwater out of the salty sea. Land creatures find pools of freshwater and running streams from the rains.

There's also the bright and powerful hot sun to think about. Some creatures hide during the day to avoid the sun, while others love the sun's heat.

We're going to check out what lives in the tide pools, beaches, and coastlines of Hawaii.

Tide Pools

Tide pools are unique habitats that are kind of like God's aquariums. They are shallow rock formations that hold ocean water. Creatures live in these solar-heated habitats because they are protected from rough waves as well as some ocean predators.

Every day, ocean tides rise and fall. At high tide, the ocean water rises, cleaning out the tide pools with fresh seawater and bringing new bits of food. At low tide, the ocean water goes down, leaving the tide pools like isolated aquariums on the shore.

Many different creatures live in tide pools across the world.

Hermit Crab

Hermit crabs have a hard exoskeleton, which means their skeleton is on the outside of their body—but their tails are soft and vulnerable. Hermit crabs find empty snail shells to live in. Hiding in a shell keeps the soft part of the crab's body safe when predators attack. Their sharp claws are another form of protection, so you'd better watch out for those!

The crab's claws have double duty. They are great for protection and are also good for capturing food on land or in the water.

Anemone

Anemones are soft-bodied creatures that have a sticky foot on one end and dangerous tentacles surrounding a mouth on the other. I say dangerous because the tentacles have venom to stun prey and pull it toward the anemone's mouth.

Anemones come in a wide range of colors and sizes.

Some anemones hitch rides on hermit crabs! The anemone helps camouflage the crab's shell and keeps predators away with its venom. In return, the anemone gets a free ride and the hermit crab's leftover food! Not a bad deal.

Spanish Dancer

Spanish Dancers are a type of sea slug with no shell. Their bright coloring is a way of telling predators that they have poison in their bodies and should NOT be eaten. Unlike other sea slugs, they can swim.

Goby Fish

Gobies are small fish. They live near the bottom of tide pools, around the sand or coral. Being a small fish means being on the bottom of the food chain. Living in a tide pool helps with survival by eliminating the threat of bigger predators that can't get in. Gobies can also jump from pool to pool.

Gobies are helpful because not only are they a food source for many ocean creatures, but they clean up their habitat by eating small plant and animal matter. Some gobies even eat parasites and dead skin off larger fish.

Gobies are the smallest in size of any fish in the world.

Beach Habitats

In Hawaii, there are three main types of beaches: white, red, and black. Each beach is made of different things and created in different ways.

Black beaches were created when lava flowed straight down into the ocean. The water cooled the superhot lava really fast. The extreme change in temperature shattered the lava into the tiny pieces that became the black sand.

Instead of lava being cooled by water, red beaches are made up of gas bubbles that were quickly cooled by air as lava exploded out of the ground. The red beaches are rich in iron. Iron gives the sand its rusty-red color.

White beaches are the most popular and common in Hawaii. This sand was not originally lava. White beaches are mostly tiny, crushed pieces of coral that were eaten by parrot fish out on the reef.

Ghost Crab

Crabs have gills that need to stay wet, so they stay in the moist and cool sand all day. By nighttime, however, they need a dunk in the ocean.

Once in the ocean, they have to watch out for predators like crab-eating fish! If they survive their nightly swim, the crabs become the predators—eating anything small enough on the beach for them to handle.

Ghost crabs clean up the beach every night by eating anything they find—including dead fish and other creatures that wash up on shore.

Ghost crabs are among the fastest creatures in the world! Crazy Cool FACT!

Coconut Palm Tree

You are likely to see palm trees on many tropical islands. There are many species of palm trees in the world. Some produce dates, some nuts, and others coconuts.

Like all plants, coconut palms need to spread their seeds to different places in case disease or disaster destroys part of the population. God carefully designed the coconut with all that it needs to safely make the trip to other shorelines.

The tough waterproof outer shell keeps the coconut afloat at sea without getting rotten. The hard shell protects the seed against the harsh sun and the jagged coral reefs it might cross to get to land. Once on land, all the rich coconut meat and juice inside give the coconut seed what it needs to grow.

Common Myna

During the day, the common mynas hop around on the ground looking for food. At night, they roost in huge groups—sometimes hundreds of them—making quite a racket.

Mynas are omnivores, which means they eat both plants and insects. These birds adapt well to where people live and benefit from the extra food they find.

Mynas are cavity nesters. This means they like to build their nests in holes. They'll build in tree holes and even holes on a building.

Mynas, part of the starling family, have been known to imitate sounds that they hear—including the human voice!

Crazy Cool FACT!

Anole Lizard

Anoles are daytime sit-and-wait hunters. They love to lie in the sun, looking for tasty insects to catch and eat. They are common in coastal cities.

A male anole is very territorial and will chase off other males that come near its home. You can identify a male by its behavior. It does little push-ups and pumps its dewlap in and out to impress females and scare other males. A dewlap is a brightly colored thin flap of skin on a lizard's throat that is hidden most of the time.

Anole lizards can change color from bright green to dark brown and all shades in between. Another chameleon-like feature is that they have turret eyes that move independently of each other.

Crazy Cool FACT!

Habitats on Hawaii

Each Hawaiian island is the peak of a volcano, and every island has both high and low areas. The Hawaiian lowlands and upcountry are very different from each other and create different habitats.

Fresh rainwater makes it possible for plant growth on these volcanic islands. Algae, mosses, and lichens are usually the first growth on lava rocks. Eventually ferns, shrubs, and trees are able to grow. Once plant life is established, more creatures can survive in an area.

Hawaiian plants and animals arrived on the islands in two different ways. Plants and animals that are considered "native species" got there without help from people. "Introduced species" got there when humans brought them to the islands on purpose or by accident.

Let's take a look at some introduced and native species as we explore Hawaii's lowlands and upcountry!

Gecko

Geckos have the ability to run up walls, across ceilings, and stick to just about any surface! They don't use sticky slime, suction-cup feet, or claws. God has given these creatures something amazing.

Geckos actually have about 500,000 microscopic hairs on each foot. Each of those hairs has thousands of microfibers on it. When the gecko spreads out these fibers, there is a charge between the molecules on the foot and on the surface. This charge draws them together for a tight grip like superstrong static cling!

The gecko's toes bend the opposite way ours do. Instead of curling in, they curl up! This allows the gecko to stick and unstick its feet 15 times a second!

Did you know that one gecko foot attached to a piece of glass is strong enough to support 88 pounds and can hang by just one toe?

Crazy Cool FACT!

Cane Toad

Cane toads are the only type of toad you will find on the Hawaiian Islands. They are most often seen around dusk and dawn when they come out to look for food. And when I say food, I mean anything that they can fit in their mouths!

Cane toads will eat slugs, spiders, insects, cockroaches, and even small lizards and frogs! In some cases, they'll eat whole mice and even dog and cat food.

Originally from Central and South America, cane toads are now in the United States, the Caribbean, the Pacific Islands, Japan, Papua New Guinea, and Australia.

Crazy Cool FACT!

Jackson's Chameleon

Jackson's chameleons are arboreal—which means they are designed for life in the trees. Their feet are made to grasp branches, and their tails are prehensile. That means it's specially designed to grab things. Jackson's chameleons can look in totally different directions at the same time. They have the biggest turret eyes of any lizard.

When a chameleon sees a tasty insect, muscle tension builds up in the tongue as both eyes focus on the target. With lightning speed, the tongue shoots out at twice the length of the chameleon's body. Just before catching the food, the tip of the tongue forms a suction cup shape and BLAM! The sticky tongue pulls back to the mouth.

Just like other chameleons, they can change color. They can be green, yellowish, brown, gray, or even bluish in color!

The tongue of a Jackson's chameleon is so powerful, that it can hold food that is 15% of its weight! That's like me holding a 24-pound burger on my tongue!

Crazy Cool FACT!

Iappy-face spiders hide under leaves and hunt or insects that land or crawl above them. When food rrives, they reach around the leaf to grab dinner!

Iod gave the members of the happy-face spider pecies all the genetic information they need to have nany different variations. How and why each one lisplays a different pattern or color is a complex opic, but it all shows the great diversity and creativity of the Creator.

Spiders are arachnids—a group of creatures that includes spiders, scorpions, mites, ticks, and daddy longlegs.

Crazy Cool FACT!

Honeycreeper

Honeycreepers are beautiful bright forest birds. They have specially designed beaks to drink nectar out of flowers.

When honeycreepers drink nectar from an ohia tree's flowers, they are doing the tree an important service. When the bird's head is in the flower, pollen dust gets on the bird's face. When the bird goes to another flower, some of that pollen dust falls off and pollinates the next flower.

Pollination is an important part of the ecosystem. It makes it possible for seeds to be produced and more trees to grow.

This is a great example of the way God designed habitats to work. The birds get food and a place to build their nest, while the tree gets pollinated and the ability to spread more of its kind.

Crazy Cool FACT!

The ohia tree is one of the first trees to take root and grow after a lava flow.

Nene Goose

The nene goose is the state bird of Hawaii, and Hawaii is the only place in the world where you can find it. God designed the nene to thrive only in the unique habitat of upcountry Hawaii.

Less webbing and strong legs help nene geese walk across the rough volcanic terrain. Less webbing also allows them to climb on shrubs to get berries. With less bodies of water around than other places in the world, it's often from the berries and the morning dew that nenes get the water they need. A more upright posture allows them to reach food that is higher off the ground.

Ninety percent of all the species on Hawaii are endemic—that means they are found nowhere else on earth.

Final Thoughts

Understanding what habitats are and how creatures live in them is very important to understanding how God's natural world works. God has called us to be stewards of his creation, which means he has put us in charge to manage and take care of his animals, plants, and habitats. Knowing how to make the right decisions when it comes to caring for creation means knowing the Creator himself and understanding the needs of plants, animals, and habitats.

Several of the animals in this book are nearly extinct because people have not been good stewards of God's creation. As God's children, we need to make sure we make the right decisions about how we live so God can see we are doing our part to care for what he has made.

Now head outside and experience the nature of God!

Acknowledgments

I want to thank my great Creator and heavenly Father for giving me this opportunity and adventure. I am very thankful for my incredibly loving family, who supported and encouraged me every step of the way—I could not have done this without you! I wish to extend appreciation to Dr. Mark Whalon and Dr. Jonathon Schramm for their input and ideas. Thanks go to the Cesere brothers, John and Dan, for their help and their wonderful photographs that are part of this book. No list could be complete without acknowledging my wonderful editor and collaborator, Mary Hassinger—thank you for being there for me!

ZONDERKIDZ

Ocean Adventures Revised

Requests for information should be addressed to:
Zonderkidz, *5300 Patterson Ave SE, Grand Rapids, Michigan 49530*

Library of Congress Cataloging-in-Publication Data

Schriemer, Peter, author.
Ocean adventures / by Peter Schriemer. – Revised.
pages cm – (Nature of God)
Audience: Ages 4 to 8.
ISBN 978-0-310-74381-1 (softcover)
1. Marine ecology—Juvenile literature. 2. Marine biology—Juvenile literature. 3. Pacific Ocean—Juvenile literature. I. Title.
QH91.16.S37 2014
578.77–dc23 2013031358

Editor: Mary Hassinger
Art direction: Cindy Davis
Interior design: Brand Navigation

Printed in China

14 15 16 /LPC/ 10 9 8 7 6 5 4 3 2

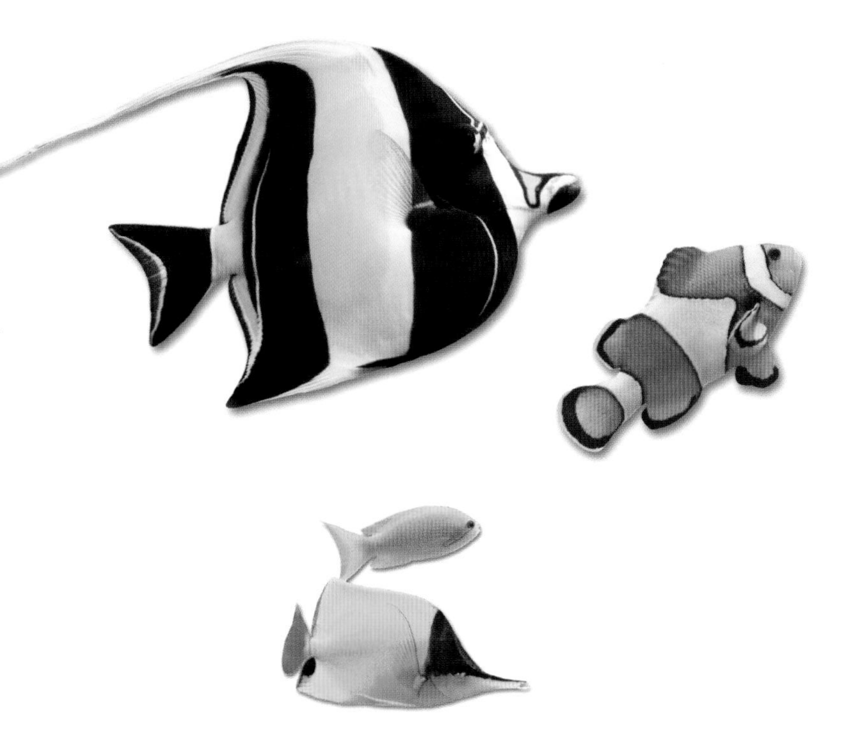